King Bidgood's in the Bathtub

WRITTEN BY
Audrey Wood

ILLUSTRATED BY
Don Wood

HARCOURT BRACE & COMPANY
SAN DIEGO   NEW YORK   LONDON

Requests for permission to make copies of any part of the work should be
mailed to: Permissions Department, Harcourt Brace & Company,
6277 Sea Harbor Drive, Orlando, Florida 32887-6777.

Library of Congress Cataloging-in-Publication Data
Wood, Audrey.
King Bidgood's in the bathtub.
Summary: Despite pleas from his court, a fun-loving
king refuses to get out of his bathtub to rule his
kingdom.
1. Children's stories, American. [1. Kings, queens,
rulers, etc.—Fiction. 2. Baths—Fiction] I. Wood,
Don, 1945– ill. II. Title.
PZ7.W846ki 1985 [E] 85-5472
ISBN 0-15-242730-9

Printed in the United States of America

I J K L

The paintings in this book were done in oil on pressed board.
The text type was set on the Linotron 202 in Clearface Roman.
The display type was photoset in Rococo.
Color separations were made by Heinz Weber, Inc., of Los Angeles, California.
Composed by Thompson Type, San Diego, California
Printed by The Eusey Press, Leominster, Massachusetts
Bound by Horowitz/Rae Book Manufacturers, Inc., Fairfield, New Jersey
Production supervision by Warren Wallerstein
Typography and binding design by Joy Chu

For Edwin Cook Brewer

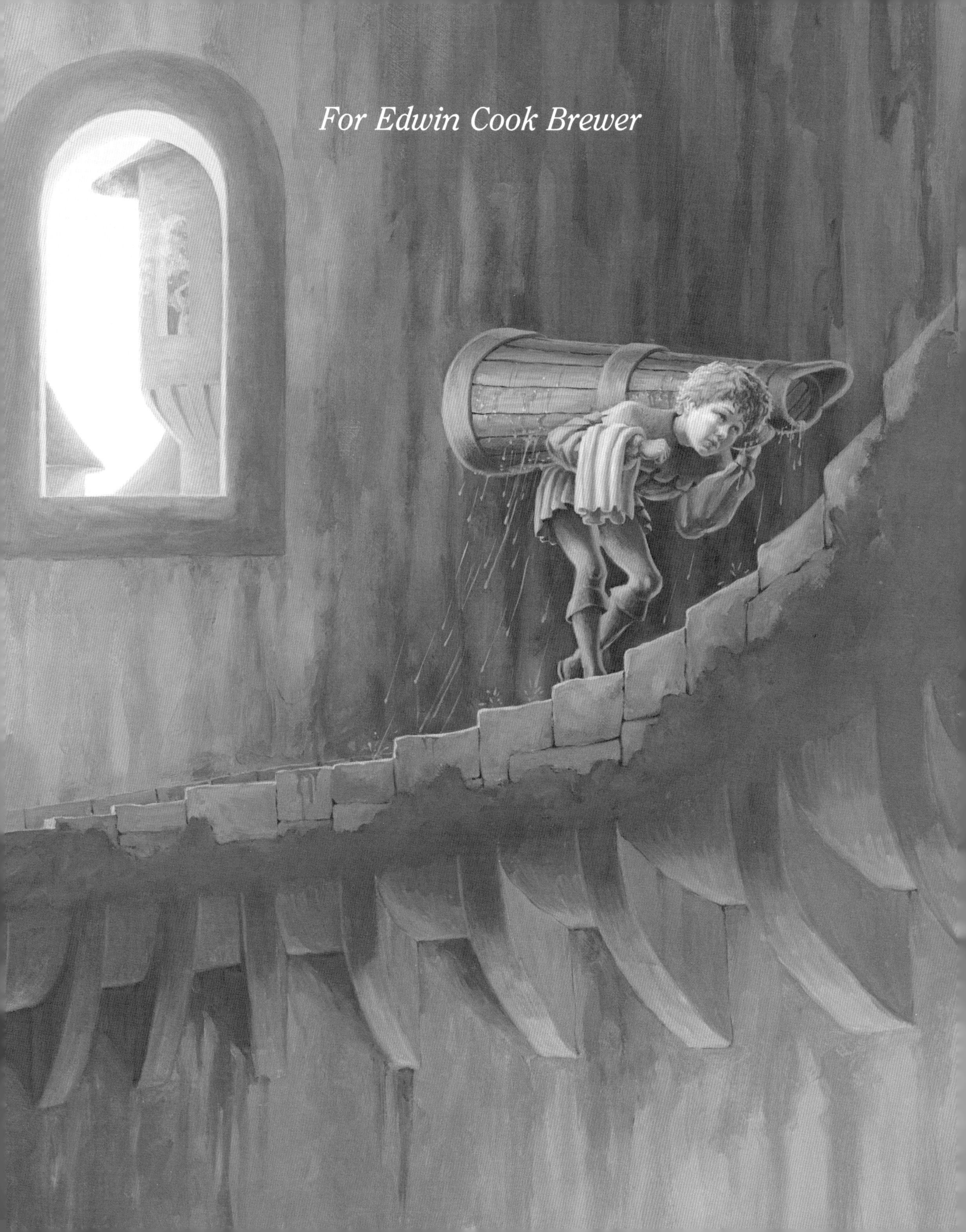

"Help! Help!" cried the Page when the sun came up.
"King Bidgood's in the bathtub, and he won't get out!
Oh, who knows what to do?"

"I do!" cried the Knight when the sun came up.
"Get out! It's time to battle!"

"Come in!" cried the King, with a boom, boom, boom.

"Today we battle in the tub!"

"Help! Help!" cried the Page when the sun got hot.
"King Bidgood's in the bathtub, and he won't get out!
Oh, who knows what to do?"

"I do!" cried the Queen when the sun got hot.
"Get out! It's time to lunch!"
"Come in!" cried the King, with a yum, yum, yum.

"Today we lunch in the tub!"

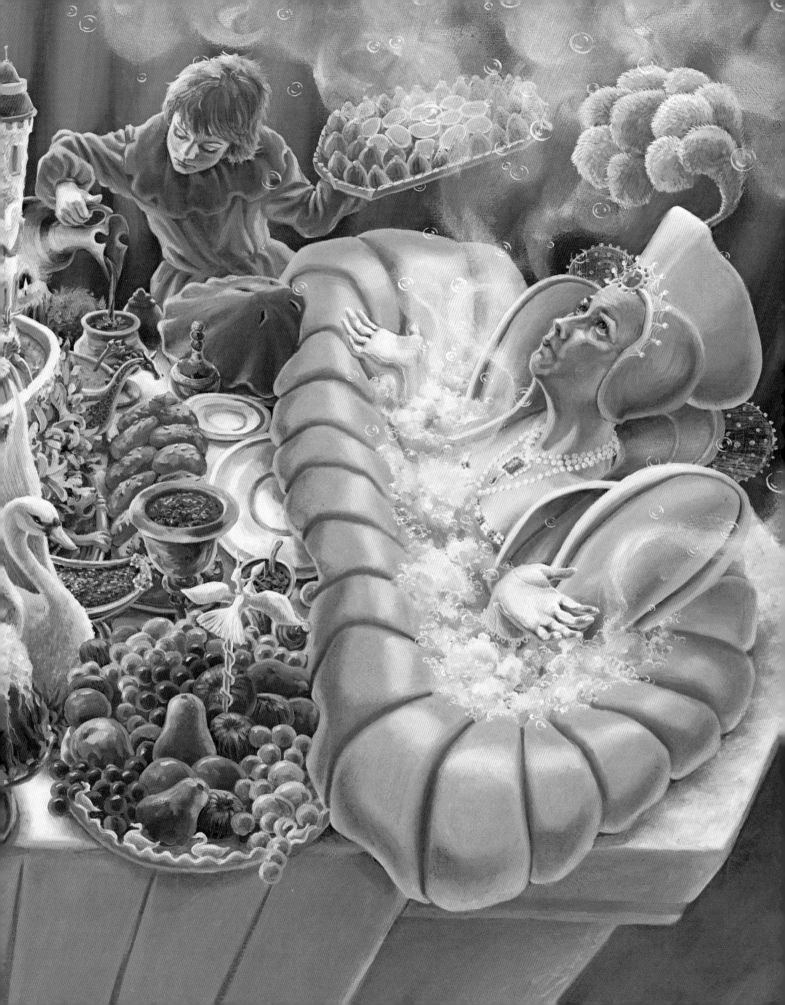

"Help! Help!" cried the Page when the sun sank low.
"King Bidgood's in the bathtub, and he won't get out!
Oh, who knows what to do?"

"I do!" cried the Duke when the sun sank low.
"Get out! It's time to fish!"
"Come in!" cried the King, with a trout, trout, trout.

"Today we fish in the tub!"

"Help! Help!" cried the Page when the night got dark.
"King Bidgood's in the bathtub, and he won't get out!
Oh, who knows what to do?"

"We do!" cried the Court when the night got dark.
"Get out for the Masquerade Ball!"
"Come in!" cried the King, with a jig, jig, jig.

"Tonight we dance in the tub!"

"Help! Help!" cried the Court when the moon shone bright.
"King Bidgood's in the bathtub, and he won't get out!
Oh, who knows what to do?
Who knows what to do?"

"I do!" said the Page when the moon shone bright,
and then he pulled the plug.

Glub, glub, glub!